SLITHERY, SQUIRMY, JOKES

by Diane Namm
illustrated by Wayne Becker

STERLING

New York / London
www.sterlingpublishing.com/kids

STERLING and the distinctive Sterling logo are registered trademarks of
Sterling Publishing Co., Inc.

Library of Congress Cataloging-in-Publication Data

Namm, Diane.
Slithery, squirmy jokes / by Diane Namm, illustrated by Wayne Becker.
p. cm. -- (Laugh-a-long readers)
Originally published: New York : Barnes & Noble Books, c2004.
ISBN-13: 978-1-4027-5003-8
ISBN-10: 1-4027-5003-X
1. Animals--Juvenile humor. 2. Wit and humor, Juvenile. I. Becker, Wayne. II. Title.
PN6231.A5N36 2004
818'.5402--dc22
2007030248

2   4   6   8   10   9   7   5   3   1

Published 2008 by Sterling Publishing Co., Inc.
387 Park Avenue South, New York, NY 10016
Originally published and © 2004 by Barnes and Noble, Inc.
Distributed in Canada by Sterling Publishing
c/o Canadian Manda Group, 165 Dufferin Street
Toronto, Ontario, Canada M6K 3H6
Distributed in the United Kingdom by GMC Distribution Services
Castle Place, 166 High Street, Lewes, East Sussex, England BN7 1XU
Distributed in Australia by Capricorn Link (Australia) Pty. Ltd.
P.O. Box 704, Windsor, NSW 2756, Australia

Written by Diane Namm
Illustrated by Wayne Becker
Designed by Jo Obarowski

Sterling ISBN-13: 978-1-4027-5003-8
ISBN-10: 1-4027-5003-X

For information about custom editions, special sales, premium and corporate purchases,
please contact Sterling Special SalesDepartment at 800-805-5489 or specialsales@sterlingpub.com.

What does a worm do when it sees a lot of corn?

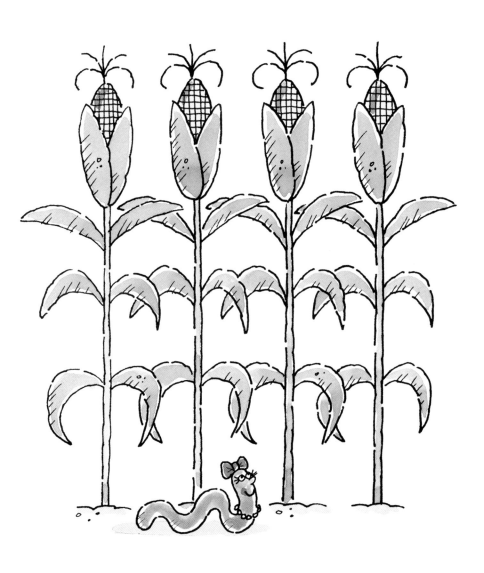

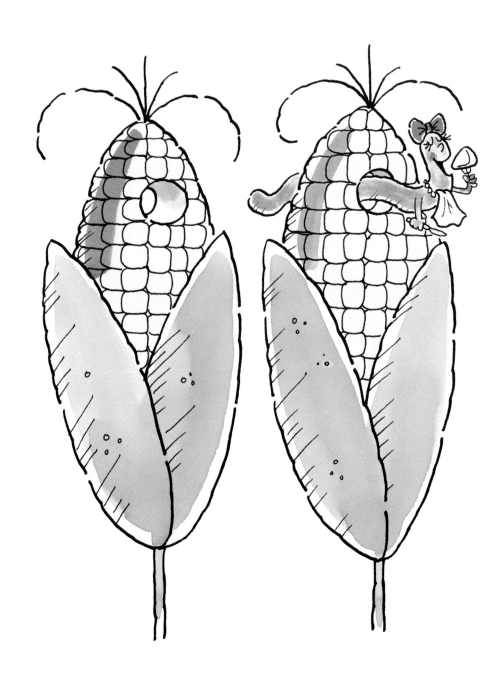

*It goes in one ear and out
the other.*

How many worms can you put in an empty can?

One. After that the can is not empty.

Why did the worm sleep late every morning?

He didn't want the early bird
to catch him.

What does a boa constrictor call his girlfriend?

His main squeeze.

Why is it hard to fool a snake?

Because you can't pull its leg.

Why is computer class a spider's favorite?

Spiders just love the web.

What do you call fifty rats
in the dark?

Scary!

How do you make a lizard laugh?

Tickle it.

What can a friendly bug give you?

A bug hug.

Why do spiders spin webs?

They don't know how to knit.

Why are spiders good at baseball?

They catch a lot of flies.

Why do bees have sticky hair?

They brush with honeycombs.

What kind of bug does a knight fight?

A dragonfly.

Why did the baby snake cry?

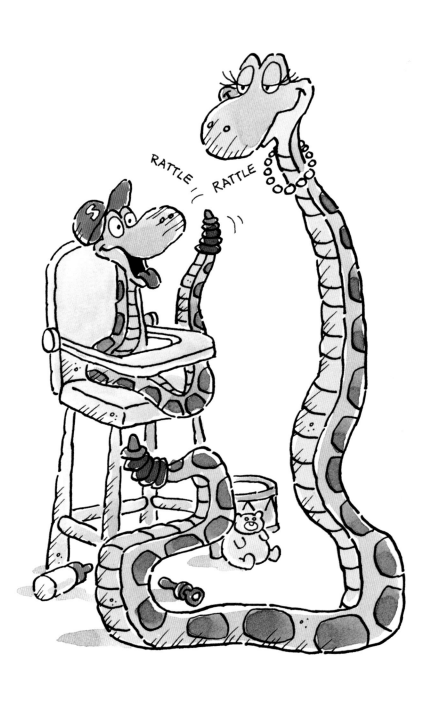

He lost his rattle.

What is worse than a snake in your bathtub?

Two snakes in your bathtub.